Jimmieboy's Snowman

and other Christmas Stories

Miles
Kelly

First published in 2015 by Miles Kelly Publishing Ltd
Harding's Barn, Bardfield End Green, Thaxted, Essex, CM6 3PX, UK

This edition printed 2018

4 6 8 10 9 7 5 3

Publishing Director Belinda Gallagher
Creative Director Jo Cowan
Editorial Director Rosie Neave
Senior Editor Sarah Parkin
Design Manager Joe Jones
Production Elizabeth Collins, Jennifer Brunwin-Jones
Reprographics Stephan Davis, Jennifer Cozens, Thom Allaway
Assets Lorraine King

ISBN 978-1-78209-830-0

Printed in China

British Library Cataloguing-in-Publication Data
A catalogue record for this book is available from the British Library

ACKNOWLEDGEMENTS
The publishers would like to thank the following artists who have contributed to this book:

Front cover: Simona Sanfilippo (Plum Pudding Illustration Agency)

Inside illustrations:
Decorative frame Rachel Cloyne (Pickled Ink)
Scrooge Celebrates Christmas Simona Sanfilippo (Plum Pudding Illustration Agency)
Jimmieboy's Snowman Charlotte Cooke (The Bright Agency)
Mr Dog Plays Santa Claus Antonia Woodward (Plum Pudding Illustration Agency)
Katy and Clover's Christmas Natalia Moore (Advocate Art)

Made with paper from a sustainable forest

www.mileskelly.net

Contents

Scrooge Celebrates Christmas

An extract from *A Christmas Carol*
by Charles Dickens

*Ebenezer Scrooge has been shown by three ghosts what
a mean man he has been, especially to his clerk, Bob Cratchit,
and his nephew Fred. Scrooge has always hated Christmas, but
the ghosts have shown him what a wonderful season it is.
Now he has woken up, determined to do better.*

"*I* don't know what day of the month it is!" said Scrooge. "I don't know how long I've been among the Spirits. I don't know anything. I'm quite a baby. Never mind.

I don't care. I'd rather be a baby. Hallo!
Whoop! Hallo here!"

He was checked by the churches ringing
out the lustiest peals he had ever heard.
Clash, clang, hammer! Ding, dong! Dong, ding!
Hammer, clang, clash! Oh, glorious, glorious!

Running to the window, he opened it and
put out his head. No fog, no mist – clear,
bright, jovial, stirring. Cold – cold, piping
for the blood to dance to. Golden sunlight,
heavenly sky, sweet fresh air, merry bells.
Oh, glorious! Glorious!

"What's today?" cried Scrooge, calling
downwards to a boy in Sunday clothes.

"Today?" replied the boy. "Why, it's
Christmas Day."

"It's Christmas Day!" said Scrooge. "I
haven't missed it. Hallo, my fine fellow!"

"Hallo!" returned the boy.

"Do you know the Poulterer's, in the next street but one, at the corner?" Scrooge asked the boy.

"I should hope I did," replied the lad.

"An intelligent boy!" said Scrooge. "A remarkable boy! Do you know whether they've sold the turkey that was hanging up there? Not the little prize one – the big one?"

"What, the one as big as me?" returned the boy.

"What a delightful boy!" said Scrooge. "It's a pleasure to talk to him. Yes, my boy!"

"It's hanging there now," replied the boy.

"Go and buy it, and tell 'em to bring it here," said Scrooge. "Come back with the man, and I'll give you a shilling. Come back with him in less than five minutes and I'll give you half a crown!"

The boy was off like a shot. "I'll send it to Bob Cratchit's!" whispered Scrooge, rubbing his hands, and splitting with a laugh. "He shan't know who sends it."

The boy returned, staggering under the weight of the enormous turkey!

"Why, it's impossible to carry that to Camden Town," said Scrooge. "You must have a cab."

The chuckle with which he said this, and the chuckle with which he paid for the turkey, and the chuckle with which he paid for the cab, and the chuckle with which he paid the boy, were only exceeded by the chuckle with which he sat down breathless in his chair again, and chuckled till he cried.

He dressed himself all in his best, and

at last got out into the streets. The people were by this time pouring forth and Scrooge regarded every one with a delighted smile. He looked so pleasant, that three or four good-humoured fellows said, "Good morning, sir! A Merry Christmas to you!"

He went to church, and walked about the streets, and watched the people hurrying to and fro, and patted children on the head, and conversed with beggars. He had never dreamed that any walk – that anything – could give him such happiness. In the afternoon he turned his steps towards his nephew's house.

He passed the door a dozen times, before he had the courage to go up and knock. But then he made a dash and did it.

"Is your master at home, my dear?" said Scrooge to the girl. Nice girl!

"Yes, sir."

"Where is he, my love?" said Scrooge.

"He's in the dining room, sir, along with mistress," the girl replied.

"Thank'ee. He knows me," said Scrooge. "I'll go in, my dear."

He turned the handle of the dining room door gently, and sidled his face in, round the door.

"Fred!" said Scrooge.

"Why bless my soul!" cried Fred, "who is that?"

"It's I. Your uncle Scrooge. I have come to dinner. Will you let me in, Fred?"

Let him in! It is a mercy Fred didn't shake his arm off. He was made to feel at home in five minutes. Wonderful party, wonderful games, wonderful happiness!

But he was early at the office next morning. Oh, he was early there. If he could only be there first, and catch Bob Cratchit coming late! That was the thing he had set his heart upon.

And he did it, yes, he did! The clock struck nine. No Bob. A quarter past. No Bob. He was eighteen minutes and a half behind his time. Scrooge sat with his door wide open, that he might see him come in.

Bob's hat was off, before he opened the door, his comforter too. He was on his stool in a jiffy, driving away with his pen, as if he

were trying to overtake nine o'clock.

"Hallo!" growled Scrooge. "What do you mean by coming here at this time of day?"

"I am very sorry, sir," said Bob. "I am behind my time."

"You are?" repeated Scrooge. "Yes. I think you are. Step this way, sir, if you please."

"It's only once a year, sir," pleaded Bob. "It shall not be repeated. I was making rather merry yesterday, sir."

"Now, I'll tell you what, my friend," said Scrooge. "I am not going to stand this sort of thing any longer. And therefore," he continued, leaping from his stool, "and therefore I am about to raise your salary!"

Bob trembled.

"A Merry Christmas, Bob!" said Scrooge, with an earnestness that could not be mistaken, as he clapped him on the back.

"A merrier Christmas, Bob, my good fellow, than I have given you, for many a year! I'll raise your salary, and endeavour to assist your struggling family, and we will discuss your affairs this very afternoon."

Scrooge was better than his word. He did it all, and infinitely more. He became as good a friend, as good a master, and as good a man, as the good old city knew, or any other good old city in the good old world.

Jimmieboy's Snowman

By John Kendrick Bangs

The snow had been falling fast for almost forty-eight hours, and Jimmieboy was almost crazy with delight. His father had made him a snowman with shoe buttons for eyes and a battered old hat on his head.

After the snowman was finished, Jimmieboy shouted in great glee, and then he ran up into his bedroom to rest.

After a while Jimmieboy ran to the

window to see if the snowman was all right, and he was much surprised to discover that he wasn't there at all. The snowman couldn't have melted, that was certain, for the air was colder than it had been when the snowman was put up.

'It's strange!' thought Jimmieboy. 'He was there ten minutes ago.'

And then the doorbell rang, and Jimmieboy went to the door and opened it. There was the snowman!

"Won't you come in?" asked Jimmieboy.

The snowman stared at Jimmieboy and then he said:

"Indeed, I'll enter not that door,
I've tried it once or twice before."
"Didn't you like it?" Jimmieboy asked.
"Oh, yes, I liked it well enough,
Although it used me pretty rough.
I lost a nose and foot and ear,
Last time I happened to come here."
"Do you always speak in rhyme?" asked
Jimmieboy, surprised.

"Always, except when I speak in prose,"
said the snowman. "But say, don't stand
there with the door open letting all the heat
out into the world. If you want to talk to
me, come outside."

"Very well," said Jimmieboy. "I'll come, if
you'll wait until I bundle up a little so as to
keep warm."

"All right, I'll wait," the snowman
answered. "I'll take you up to where I live

and introduce you to my boys if you like – only hurry. If a thaw should set in we might have trouble."

The snowman smiled happily as Jimmieboy came out, and then the two of them went off up the road together.

"I'm glad you weren't offended with me because I wouldn't go in and sit down in your house," said the snowman. "I had a very narrow escape thirty winters ago, when I was young and didn't know any better. A small boy asked me to go into his house. I said all right, and in I went, never thinking that the house was hot and that I'd be in danger of melting away. The boy got out his picture books and we sat down before a blazing log fire. Suddenly the boy turned white as I was, and cried out, 'What have you done with your leg?'

"The minute I tried to rise and hop off on the search I discovered that my other leg was gone too!"

"How dreadful," Jimmieboy said.

"It was fearful," returned the snowman, "but that wasn't half. I raised my hand to my forehead when off dropped my right arm, and as I reached out with my left to pick it up again, that dropped off too. Then the boy cried out, 'Why, I know what's the matter. You are melting away!'

"He was right. Fortunately, as my neck began to go and my head rolled off the chair onto the floor, the boy picked it up – it was all that was left of me – and threw it out of the window."

"Do you live near here?" asked Jimmieboy, as he trudged along at the snowman's side.

"When summer comes I move up to the North Pole," replied the snowman.

Jimmieboy peered curiously along the road, at the far end of which he could see a huge mound of snow.

"Do you live in that?" he asked.

"Yes," the snowman replied. "The house part of it is always as cold as ice – it's cooled by a special kind of refrigerator I had put in, which consumes about half a tonne of ice each week. Once in a while my boys run in the sun and get warmed through, but I dose 'em up with ice water and cold cream and they soon get chilled again. But come, shall we go in now?"

By this time they had reached the side of the snowdrift, and Jimmieboy was pleased to see a door at one side of it. This the snowman opened, and they entered together a marvellously beautiful garden, glistening with frosty flowers and snow-clad trees. At the end of the garden was a little white house that looked like the icing on Jimmieboy's birthday cake. As they approached it, a dozen small-sized snow boys rushed out and began to pelt the snowman and Jimmieboy with snowballs.

"Hold up, boys," cried the snowman. "I've brought a friend home to see you."

The boys stopped at once, and Jimmieboy was introduced to them. They showed him wondrous snow toys, among which were rocking horses, railway trains

and soldiers – all made of the same soft fleecy substance from which the snowman and his children were constructed.

When Jimmieboy had played for a long time with these, they gave him caramels and cream cakes, also made of snow.

After this the boys invited him out to sledge, and he went along with them. It took his breath away the first time he went down, but when he got used to it he found the sport delightful. But he was glad when a voice from the little white house called to the children to return.

"Come in now, boys," it said. "It is getting too warm for you to stay out."

The snowman looked a little anxious, Jimmieboy thought, but he supposed this was because the littlest snow boy had overheated himself at his play, and had come in minus two fingers and an ear.

It was not this, however, that bothered him, as Jimmieboy found out in a few minutes. For the snowman simply restored the missing fingers and the ear by making a new lot for the little fellow out of a handful of snow he got from the garden. The real cause of the snowman's anxiety came out when he called Jimmieboy to one side.

"You must go home right away," he said. "I'm sorry, but we have got to fly just as hard as we can or we are lost."

"But—" said Jimmieboy.

"Don't ask for reasons," returned the snowman, gathering his little snow boys together and rushing off with them. "Just read that and you'll see. Farewell."

Jimmieboy picked up the thing the snowman had told him to read. It was a

newspaper, and at the top was an announcement in huge letters:

WARM WEATHER TONIGHT WISE SNOWMEN WILL MOVE NORTH AT ONCE

When Jimmieboy saw this he knew right away why he had been deserted. He walked to the front door and opened it, and what do you suppose it opened into?

It opened into Jimmieboy's bedroom, and when the door closed after him, lo and behold it wasn't there!

Nor was the snowman to be found the next morning. There wasn't even a sign of the shoe button eyes or the battered hat, as there certainly would have been had he melted instead of run away.

Mr Dog Plays Santa Claus

An extract from *How Mr Rabbit Lost his Tail*
by Albert Bigelow Paine

*Mr Dog lives close to the Hollow Tree,
the home of his woodland animal friends.*

Once upon a time the Robin and Turtle and Squirrel and Jack Rabbit had all gone home for the winter, and nobody was left in the Hollow Tree except the 'Coon and 'Possum and the Old Black Crow. Of course the others used to come back and

visit them pretty often, and Mr Dog, too.

Mr Dog told them things they had never heard of before, things that he'd learned at Mr Man's house, and maybe that's one reason why they got to liking him so well.

He told them about Santa Claus, for one thing, and how the old fellow came down the chimney on Christmas Eve to bring presents to Mr Man and his children, who always hung up their stockings for them. And Mr Dog said that once he had hung up his stocking, too, and got a nice bone in it.

Well, the Hollow Tree people had never heard of Santa Claus. They thought if they hung up their stockings he'd come there, too, and that's what they decided to do.

They talked about it a great deal, and Mr 'Possum looked over all his stockings to pick out the biggest one, and Mr Crow

made himself a new pair
on purpose.

When Mr Dog
heard about it he
wanted to laugh
right out. You see, he
knew Santa Claus
never went anywhere
except to Mr Man's house. But Mr Dog
did not want the Hollow Tree people to be
disappointed. He liked them all, and when
he had thought about that a minute, he
made up his mind to play Santa Claus!

Well, he had to work pretty hard to get
things ready. He found some long wool
out in Mr Man's barn for his white beard,
and he put some that wasn't so long on the
edges of his overcoat and boot tops, and
around an old hat. Then he borrowed a big

sack he found out there, too, and fixed it up to swing over his back, just as he had seen Santa Claus do in the pictures.

He had a lot of nice things to take along. Three tender young chickens he'd borrowed from Mr Man, for one thing, and then he bought some new neckties for the Hollow Tree folks, and a big, striped candy cane for each one. He had even more things than that, and when he started out, all dressed up like Santa Claus, his bag was pretty heavy.

Mr Dog was glad enough to get there and find the latch string out. He set his bag down to rest a minute before climbing the stairs, and then he opened the door softly and listened. He didn't hear a thing except Mr Crow and Mr 'Coon and Mr 'Possum breathing pretty low, and he knew they might wake up any minute.

So he slipped up as easy as anything, and when he got to the big parlour room there were the stockings, all hung up in a row, and a card with a name on it over each one.

So then he opened his bag, took down the stockings and filled them. He put in mixed candy and nuts and little things first, and then the candy canes, so they would show at the top. They looked fine! Mr Dog forgot all about them waking up, and sat down in a chair to look at the stockings.

It was a nice rocking chair, and over in a dark corner where they wouldn't see him, even if one of them did wake up and stick his head out of his room. Mr Dog rocked softly, and looked at the nice stockings, and thought how pleased they'd be in the morning, and how tired he was. He was so tired he didn't feel a bit like starting home,

and by and by Mr Dog went sound asleep right there in his chair.

Even when it began to get light, Mr Dog just slept right on, he was that tired.

Then the door of Mr 'Possum's room opened and he poked out his head. Then the door of Mr 'Coon's room opened and he poked out his head. Then the door of Mr Crow's room opened and he poked out his head. They all looked towards the stockings, and Mr 'Coon said all at once, "Oh, there's something in my stocking!"

And then Mr Crow said, "Oh, there's something in my stocking, too!"

And Mr 'Possum said, "Oh, there's something in all our stockings!"

And with that they gave a great hurrah all together, and rushed out and grabbed their stockings. They turned around just in

time to see Mr Dog jump straight up out of his chair, for he did not know where he was.

"Oh, there's Santa Claus himself!" they all shouted together, and made a rush for their rooms, for they were scared almost to death. Then it all dawned on Mr Dog in a second, and he started to laugh. And when they heard Mr Dog laugh they knew him right away, and they all came up and looked at him, and he had to tell just what he'd done and everything.

So they emptied out their stockings on the floor and ate some of the presents and looked at the others, until they almost forgot about breakfast, just as children do on Christmas morning.

Katy and Clover's Christmas

An extract from *What Katy Did at School*
by Susan Coolidge

*It is Christmas Eve, and Katy, Clover and their friend
Rose Red are at a boarding school, run by the strict Mrs Nipson.
The girls stay at school for Christmas, and though they are all
hoping their parents will have sent them boxes full of
Christmas presents, nothing has arrived.*

"*I*t isn't much like merry Christmas,"
sighed Clover to herself, as she looked
up at the window and saw great snowflakes
whirling by. Then Mrs Nipson came in.

"Miss Carr, come here for a moment, if you please."

Clover, wondering, followed her.

"A parcel has arrived for you, and a box," said Mrs Nipson. "I will have the nails removed, and both of them placed in your room, but I expect you to refrain from examining them until tomorrow."

"Very well, ma'am," said Clover.

Study hour seemed unusually long that night. The minute it was over, the sisters ran to No. 2. There stood the boxes, a big wooden one and a small paper one. It was almost more than the girls could do to obey orders and not peep.

"I feel something hard," announced Clover, inserting a finger under the lid.

"Oh, do you?" cried Katy. Then, making a heroic effort, she jumped into the bed.

"It's the only way," she said. "Let's get to sleep as fast as we can, so as to make morning come quicker."

Katy dreamed of home. Perhaps it was that which made her wake so early. It was not five o'clock, and the room was dark. She lay perfectly still, for hours as it seemed. Then she could wait no longer, but crept out of bed and, raising the lid, put in her hand. Something crumby and sugary met it, and there, fitting on her finger, was a round cake with a hole.

"Oh! It's one of Debby's jumbles!"

"Where? What? Give me one too!" cried Clover. The two lay nibbling the jumbles and talking about home till morning.

Breakfast was half an hour later than usual, which was comfortable. As soon as it was over, the girls proceeded to unpack their box. The day was so cold that they wrapped themselves in shawls, and Clover put on a hood and thick gloves. Rose Red, passing the door, recommended that she should add an umbrella.

"Come in," cried the sisters, "and help us open our box."

"Oh, by the way, you have a box, haven't you?" said Rose, who was perfectly aware of the important fact, and had presented herself with the hope of being asked to look on. "Thank you, but perhaps I shall be in your way."

"You humbug!" said Clover. "You know you came on purpose!"

"Did I? Well, perhaps I did," laughed Rose. Then Katy lifted off the lid.

"Just look here!" she said.

The top of the box was mostly taken up with four square paper boxes, round which parcels of all shapes and sizes were wedged. One was of jumbles, another of ginger snaps, a third of crullers, and the fourth contained a big loaf of frosted plum cake.

"I never imagined anything so nice," declared Rose, with her mouth full of jumble. "As for those snaps, they're simply perfect. What can be in all those fascinating bundles? Do hurry and open one, Katy."

Dear little Elsie! The first two bundles opened were hers, a white hood for Katy and a blue one for Clover, both of her own knitting. The girls were enchanted. They tried them on and spent so much time in admiring them that Rose grew impatient.

"I declare," she cried, "it isn't any of my funeral, I know, but if you don't open another parcel soon, I shall certainly fall to myself."

"Very well," said Katy, laying aside her hood, with one final glance. "Take out a bundle, Clover. It's your turn."

What fun it was opening those bundles! The girls made a long business of it, taking out but one at a time, exclaiming, admiring and exhibiting to Rose, before they began upon another. They laughed, they joked, but I do not think it would have taken

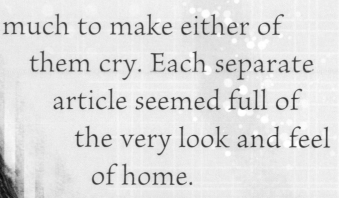

much to make either of them cry. Each separate article seemed full of the very look and feel of home.

"What can this be?" said Katy, as she unrolled a paper and disclosed a pretty round box. She opened it and gave a cry. "Oh Clovy! Such a lovely thing! It's from Papa, of course it's from Papa."

The 'lovely thing' was a long slender chain for Katy's watch, worked in fine yellow gold. Clover's joy knew no bounds when further search revealed another box with a precisely similar chain for herself.

"There never was such a papa in the world!" they said.

"Yes, there is. Mine is just as good," declared Rose. "I never saw such pretty chains in my life – never. Katy, I'm dying to know what is in the blue parcel."

The blue parcel contained a pretty blue ribbon for Clover. There was a pink one also, with a pink ribbon for Katy.

Everybody had thought of the girls. Old Mary sent them each a yard measure, and Miss Finch, a thread-case, stocked with differently coloured cottons. Alexander had cracked a bag full of hickory nuts.

Never was such a wonderful box. It appeared to have no bottom whatever. Under the presents were parcels of figs, prunes, almonds, raisins, candy, and under those, apples and pears. There seemed no

end to the surprises. But at last all were out.

"Now," said Katy, "I want you to help divide the other things, and make some packages for the girls. They are all disappointed not to have their boxes. I should like to have them share ours. Wouldn't you, Clover?"

"Yes. I was just going to propose it."

So Clover, Rose and Katy sorted ginger snaps and almonds and sugar plums. None of the snowed-up boxes got through till Monday, so except for Katy and Clover the school would have had no Christmas treat.

'The Carrs' Box' was always quoted as an example of what papas and mammas could accomplish, when they were of the right sort, and wanted to make schoolgirls happy.

Distributing their treasures kept Katy and Clover so busy that it was not until

after dinner that they found time to open the smaller box.

The box was full of flowers – roses, red geranium leaves and white carnations. Cousin Helen had sent them. And underneath, sewed to the box, that they might not shake about, were two flat parcels wrapped in tissue paper. They were glove cases, of quilted silk, delicately scented, one white, and one lilac, and to each was pinned a note, wishing the girls a Merry Christmas.

"How awfully good people are!" said Clover. "I do think we ought to be the best girls in the world."